DOUBLE TROUBLE

"I wanna be the Swamp Monster, with icky green stuff hanging down from my arms," said the little girl. She curled her fingers like claws and marched stiff-legged around the room moaning.

The little boy came charging back. "Muscle Man can beat the Swamp Monster!" He danced around his sister, making muscles.

"Swamp Monster!" she shouted.

"Muscle Man!"

"SWAMP MONSTER!"

"MUSCLE MAN!"

The Super Squad shook their heads. This job wasn't going to be as easy as they'd thought.

COSTUME PARTY

Jennie Abbott
Illustrated by Mary Badenhop

Troll Associates

Library of Congress Cataloging-in-Publication Data

Abbott, Jennie.
    Costume party
                (The Super Squad)
        Summary: In their continuing efforts to make a million dollars,
the members of the Super Squad take on the job of designing and
constructing costumes for two sets of twins for the annual Founder's
Day costume award.
        ISBN 0-8167-1189-5 (lib. bdg.)   ISBN 0-8167-1190-9 (pbk.)
        [1. Costume—Fiction.   2. Moneymaking projects—Fiction.
3. Twins—Fiction.]   I. Badenhop, Mary, ill.   II. Title.
III. Series.
PZ7.A156Co   1988
[Fic]—dc19   87-14987

A TROLL BOOK, published by Troll Associates,
Mahwah, NJ 07430

Copyright © 1988 by Troll Associates, Mahwah, New Jersey

Printed in the United States of America.

10   9   8   7   6   5   4   3   2   1

COSTUME PARTY

Chapter
1

Three members of the Super Squad waited expectantly in Marci Arnold's basement. This week's meeting was going to be pretty exciting. Finally Marci entered the room. "I guess we all know that Founder's Day is coming up soon," she began. "And that means—"

"The Founder's Day parade at Riverview Park!" cried Annie Lewis, her green eyes sparkling. Every year, the entire town turned out wearing costumes to compete for the Thaddeus Parker Awards. Old Thaddeus had founded the town of Riverview. And the one thing he'd loved was costume parties.

"Yeah," said Carrie Young, shaking back her blond hair. "Riverview will look like a giant masquerade party. And that doesn't count all the parties going on inside the houses."

"Speaking of parties," Nicole Tucker spoke up. "I guess that's why we're having this meeting."

Marci stood staring at them with her mouth open and her horn-rimmed glasses slipping down her nose. "No," she said. "That's not why we're having this meeting."

"But you said that Founder's Day was coming, and we all know what that means—parties!" Nicole said.

"It means there'll be lots of work," Marci corrected, peering over the tops of her glasses. "Lots of odd jobs for us to do."

"I don't know," said Carrie. "It seems like all the jobs we do are odd."

"You said it!" Annie giggled, her red hair bouncing.

Marci could feel her cheeks turning red. "Our jobs might have been odd," she said, "but they earned lots of money for our Millionaire's Fund."

"So if we've got lots of money," Nicole asked, "why not spend a little and throw a great party? It could be the best ever—with great food and decorations and lots of our friends. We'll be the talk of the school."

"I don't believe you!" Marci said to Nicole. "If we left it to you, there wouldn't be a Millionaire's Fund left! I spend hours thinking of ways to invest our money. And in a few minutes, you come up with ideas to spend it all."

"Not all," said Nicole. "Just some so we can have a good time. There's more to life than making investments and calculating interest, Marci. What about having some fun?"

"Fun? *Fun?*" Marci's voice rose. "What do you call all the things we've been doing lately? We saw three movies in two weeks. And what about skating and the ice-cream party last weekend? Have you forgotten the school dance and the picnic the weekend before? And let's not leave out the bike trip—"

"Okay, okay," Nicole cut in. "I get the point. We *have* done a lot lately." She walked around the room, then threw herself dramatically into the chair. "But wouldn't it be great to have the hottest party for Founder's Day? Besides, it's only money."

"Sure," said Marci. "And the only reason we set up the Super Squad was to *make money*. With your ideas, we wouldn't have a dime left in the Fund."

"Well, maybe a dime," said Carrie.

Annie giggled, and even Marci couldn't help smiling. Everyone knew Nicole was pretty bad when it came to saving money.

Nicole shrugged. "Well, I still think a party would be pretty neat."

"Why can't we do both?" said Carrie, sticking her hands in her hooded sweatshirt. "Marci, you just said this would be a busy time for us. So why can't we take part of the money we earn on our next job and invest it, and use the rest for the party?"

"I think that's a great idea," said Annie with a smile.

9

Marci shrugged. "It'd be smarter to invest all the money. But maybe a party isn't such a bad idea."

"What do you say, Nicole?" Carrie asked.

Running her fingers through her shoulder-length brown hair, Nicole grinned. "Well, you know me. I love parties. And I guess investing some money is a good idea, too. And I'll try not to go overboard."

Carrie sighed. "Well, that sounds settled. Now, what about our next job?"

"I said there'd be lots of odd jobs," Marci said. "But two days ago, I think I got the best." She held up her notes. "We got a call from Mrs. Williams—she lives in that big wooden house on Grant Street. Well, she has four kids, and she wants us to make their costumes for Founder's Day."

"Costumes?" Nicole's face became thoughtful. "How much is it worth?"

Marci smiled. "Mrs. Williams is going to pay us eighty dollars. Twenty for each costume. Not bad, huh?"

"I think it will be fun," said Carrie. "I could go to the library and get some books on how to make costumes. We could do all sorts of crazy things, with crepe paper and glitter—maybe even papier-mâché."

"What does Mrs. Williams want us to do, exactly?" Annie asked.

"She wants each costume to be one of a kind. She says her kids are tired of being the same things every year. You know—witches, fairies, or clowns."

11

"I know," Carrie said. "Remember the time we all dressed up as ghosts?"

"Anyway," Marci continued, "Mrs. Williams doesn't have the time to make costumes herself. So that's where we come in. We're supposed to make the best Founder's Day costumes ever. Maybe even help one of the kids win a prize at the parade."

"You know," Nicole said from her chair, "this job may even help us. It could give us some ideas for costumes to wear to our own party. We should look great, since I'm inviting all the cute guys from school."

"I thought you said you weren't going to go over-board," said Marci. "Just how many kids do you plan on inviting?"

Annie looked at her watch. "Let's not talk about the party right now," she said quickly. "We should be thinking about the job. How old are the Williams kids? We ought to start thinking up some ideas."

Marci riffled through her notes. "One is seven, and one is nine."

"What about the other two?" asked Carrie.

"I don't seem to have them written down," said Marci, puzzled. She shrugged her shoulders. "Anyway, we'll find out tomorrow. I told Mrs. Williams we'd be there right after school. Is that okay with everyone?"

Annie looked at her watch again. "I—I guess so." She didn't look very happy.

"Then I'd say the meeting is over," Marci said.

"But we haven't even talked about the party," Nicole burst out. "We have to decide who we're inviting, what we ought to buy—there's really not much time, you know."

"Since the party is your idea, I think you should plan it," Marci said. "After all, we're going to be busy with those costumes."

"No fair," complained Nicole. "I can't do it alone!"

"We'll help," said Carrie. "Just make up some lists —you know, who to invite and what food we'll need. Things like that. We can talk about it in a few days, and get organized. By then we'll have a jump on these costumes."

"Okay." Nicole sighed. "But you promise to help when it comes time for buying stuff."

"Sure," said Marci. "Just remember, don't get carried away."

"All right, all right," said Nicole, pulling on her jacket.

Annie had already picked up her books and was racing up the basement stairs. "Sorry," she called. "I've got to run."

Carrie watched her leave. "Have you noticed?" she asked. "For the last couple of weeks, Annie always seems to be rushing off somewhere. I wonder what's up."

Marci shrugged. "She hasn't mentioned anything to me."

Nicole grinned. "Maybe it's a boy!"

"I don't know," Carrie said as they started up the stairs. "It's turning into a real mystery, though. A real mystery."

Chapter
2

Marci broke into a run on the last block to the Williams's house. She stopped, breathless, at the edge of the old-fashioned fence. The house was big and rambling, with a wide porch along the front.

Standing in front of the gate was Annie, looking at her watch.

"Am I on time?" Marci asked, grinning.

Annie looked up quickly. "Uh, yeah. Where are the others?"

Marci just shrugged. "What a day! First I left my math book home, and then we had a surprise quiz. I also forgot my lunch. So I went up to the science room to take care of my plant project during lunch period. And guess what? All my plants were dead—even my control. I'm back at square one."

"Well, look at the bright side," Annie said. "I think this job will be a piece of cake."

"Don't mention food," Marci moaned, holding her stomach. "I'm starving."

"You should have eaten some lunch," said a voice from behind them. Marci and Annie turned to see Carrie and Nicole walking up. Both of them carried a stack of books.

"We stopped off at the library," Carrie explained. "And we checked out all these books on costume design. It's more complicated than I thought."

"Oh, it's not too bad if you know how to sew," said Nicole. "I brought some fashion magazines, too. You never know where an idea will come from."

"Great," said Marci. "We may as well get started."

"Right," Annie agreed. "I have a lot of things to do."

Marci rang the doorbell. A few seconds later, a woman wearing an apron answered. Her light-brown hair was mussed, and one side was much grayer than the other.

"Hi, I'm Marci Arnold. These are my friends, Nicole Tucker, Annie Lewis, and Carrie Young. You called us about the costume job."

"Right," said the lady, shaking hands with Marci. "Uh-oh."

Marci stared at her hand. It had turned white.

"Sorry," said Mrs. Williams, dusting Marci's hand off with her apron. "It's flour. I've been getting it all over everything this afternoon."

"I think some got in your hair," said Nicole with a grin.

"My—" Mrs. Williams stopped as her hand went to her hair. "Well, you can see how that happened." She laughed. "I'm Carol Williams. And I'm also the owner and chief cook of Carol's Caterers."

"You're the lady who cooks for all the parties," said Nicole.

"That's right," said Mrs. Williams, leading them into the house. "With all the parties around Founder's Day, I'm super busy. That's why I need your help."

She led them into the living room. It was cluttered with papers, cookbooks, and toys. Mrs. Williams sighed as she looked around. "Please excuse the mess. With four little ones, it's almost impossible to keep things in order. They're always one step ahead of me."

Upstairs, they heard the thumping of footsteps.

"I'll be right back," said Mrs. Williams. "After I round up the troops, I'll bring in some snacks."

Marci and Annie cleared a space on the blue-flowered love seat. Carrie and Nicole sat on over-stuffed club chairs.

The footsteps upstairs finally ended, and two kids came clattering down the stairs. A strawberry-blond girl skidded to a halt when she spotted strangers, and a dark-haired boy behind her crashed right into her.

"Ow!" he said. Then he saw the Super Squad and got quiet, too.

"Hi, I'm Marci. What's your name?" Marci asked the girl.

"Francine." The girl blushed hard enough to hide her freckles and played with the ends of her braids.

"And what's your name?" Marci asked the boy.

"Doug." He hid behind his sister.

"We're here to help you make costumes for Founder's Day," said Nicole. "What do you want to go as?"

Little Doug suddenly found his courage. "We should all go as spacemen!" He held out an imaginary ray gun, pretending to shoot it. "NYERK! NYERK!" he yelled.

The girls looked at each other. How could that small boy make such loud noise?

"Quit it, Doug," said Francine. "We're not all wearing the same costumes again."

"Well, then, *I'm* going as a spaceman! NYERK! NNNNNYERRRRRRRRK!" Still aiming his make-believe gun, Doug ran out of the room.

"One down, three to go," Annie muttered. She looked at Francine. "What would *you* like to be?"

Francine shrugged. "I don't know. Maybe a ballerina." She got up on her toes and twirled around. Then she, too, ran out of the room.

"Well, that's not too hard," said Nicole.

Suddenly the little strawberry-blond girl ran back into the room and stared at the girls.

"You'll make a pretty little ballerina," said Carrie.

"Ballerina!" The girl shook her head. "I wanna be the Swamp Monster, with icky green stuff hanging down from my arms!" She stuck her arms straight out and crooked her fingers like claws. Then she marched stiff-legged around the room, moaning.

The little boy came charging back. "Don't worry," he said. "Muscle Man can beat the Swamp Monster! That's who I'm going to be!" He danced around his sister, making muscles.

"Swamp Monster!" she shouted.

"Muscle Man!"

"SWAMP MONSTER!"

"MUSCLE MAN!"

The girl began chasing her brother. They circled the coffee table twice, then dashed out of the room again, still screaming.

Marci shook her head. So did Carrie, Annie, and Nicole.

"This isn't going to be as easy as we thought," said Carrie.

Mrs. Williams came back into the living room, carrying a big tray. "Well, I heard you meeting my little devils. I think you need a snack."

She put the tray down on the coffee table. It held a large bottle of soda, a stack of plastic glasses, and a plate full of steaming mini-pizzas!

"I'm cooking up a big batch for Mrs. Chesterton's party tonight," Mrs. Williams explained. "So I made a few more."

Marci was the first to grab a couple of the little pizzas. She gobbled them down hungrily, trying to quiet the noise her empty stomach was making.

"This is the busiest my company has ever been," Mrs. Williams said. "I just can't find the time to work and make the costumes myself. My husband usually helps, but he's away on business for a few weeks."

"Don't worry," Marci said. "We can handle the job—as long as the kids decide what they want to be. We've met Francine and Doug, and they've both changed their minds in a couple of minutes."

She explained how the ballerina had turned into the Swamp Monster, and the spaceman had turned into Muscle Man.

"Hmmmmm," said Mrs. Williams. "We'd better get this settled." She raised her voice. "Kids! Front and center!"

Francine and Doug came running into the room. Behind them came another girl with strawberry-blond hair and another dark-haired boy.

Nicole stared. "Twins!" she said.

Mrs. Williams ruffled the kids' hair. "Yup," she said. "Two sets of them. You've met Francine and Doug. This is Megan, and this is Mike. The girls are nine, and the boys are seven."

Megan grinned, showing off a missing front tooth. "We met already. I'm gonna be the Swamp Monster."

"And I'm gonna be Muscle Man," said Mike.

"Hey, *I* wanna be the Swamp Monster," Doug butted in. "That's better than being a spaceman."

"Oh, no. You're not stealing my idea. We're all going to the parade as different things this year. Mom said so."

"But I wanna be the Swamp Monster," Doug protested. "The Swamp Monster isn't a girl."

"The Swamp Monster is an *it*," said Francine. "And it's yucky."

"Well, I don't care," Megan yelled. "I picked it first. Mom!"

"*Mom!*" yelled Doug.

Mrs. Williams shook her head. The Super Squad could see why she was hiring them for this job.

"I have an idea," Marci shouted across the noise. "There's four of us and four kids. We can each make a costume. And it will be secret—no one will know what it is."

"I choose Marci," said Doug. "She looks smart. I bet we'll have the best costume."

"And I'll take . . . you!" said Megan, grabbing Nicole's hand. "We'll show them."

Mike picked Annie, and Francine chose Carrie.

"And no cheating," said Megan fiercely. "Our costumes will be a secret."

"I'm glad that's all settled," said Mrs. Williams. "When do you want to get started?"

"Tomorrow is Saturday," Marci said. "If it's okay, we could come over then."

"Yay!" yelled the four Williams kids.

"That's fine," said Mrs. Williams. "I suppose you'll have to get supplies and things. Here's some money for that, plus half your money in advance." She handed Marci some bills.

"Thanks," said Marci, pocketing them.

Annie looked at her watch. "I think it's time we got going."

The girls got their jackets and headed for the door. "Bye, kids," they called.

"BYE!" the kids yelled back.

"See you tomorrow," said Carrie.

"Start thinking up new ideas," added Nicole.

They stepped out of the house, and down the walk to the gate.

"I think this will be a fun job—especially with twins," said Carrie. "They're so cute."

"Um, yeah," said Annie. "Can't talk, guys. I'm late!" She dashed off down the street.

Her friends stared after her. What was going on with Annie?

Chapter
3

"Calm down," Annie told herself, looking down at her bare feet. "It's not a matter of life and death."

She was sitting on a bench in the town pool's locker room, hugging herself. It wasn't because she felt cold in her bathing suit. Annie was feeling nervous.

Maybe I should just give it up, she thought. After all, I could use the time to work on Mike's costume.

She jumped to her feet. "No," she said out loud. "I said I was going to try out for the swimming team, and I will." She slammed the door of her locker shut and headed for the pool. The smell of chlorine hung over the water as Annie walked to the side of the pool. "One . . . two . . . three!"

Annie dove smoothly into the pool and began moving in quick strokes. She cut smoothly through the water, working hard at keeping her breathing even. She took a deep breath, every two strokes, as her face came out of the water.

Reaching the far end, Annie turned underwater in one smooth motion. Then she headed back the way she'd come. Back and forth she went, concentrating on her speed, pushing herself to the limit. After two more laps, she leaned against the edge of the pool, almost too tired to pull herself out.

For the past two months, she'd been practicing in secret. She wished she could tell someone about her dream of making the team. It would help to have someone able to clock her practices. But at first, she'd been embarrassed. What if she was no good?

And then there was Carrie. Carrie had always been the athlete of the group. How would she like it if Annie went out for a team?

Annie sighed as she pulled herself out of the pool and picked up her towel. Now wasn't the time to worry about that. The tryouts were a week from Monday. She'd have to worry about them, first.

Nicole sat in Marci's bedroom, leafing through a fashion magazine. She yawned loudly and looked at her watch. "Come on, Marci," she muttered. "I have things to do, too."

She had come over to Marci's house to talk about the party plans. And as she looked over the lists in her hands, Nicole was sure that Marci wouldn't be happy.

She had tried to keep the guest list down, but there were still a lot of kids to invite. And to get soda and stuff for them would be expensive. Maybe she should only show Marci the list of decorations. That wasn't too bad. If they bought them first, they could work up to the more costly lists later.

But Marci wasn't even home. Mrs. Arnold had reminded Nicole that tonight was Marci's computer class. Great. So now she had to wait for the inevitable: Marci would look over her lists and have a fit.

Nicole looked at her watch again. Marci still wouldn't be back for a while yet. Maybe it would be smarter if she just left. . . .

Brrrrrng! Brrrrrng!

Nicole stood up when she heard the ringing phone.

Brrrrrng!

Marci's mom had given her her own phone when Super Squad business began to expand.

"I guess I should get it," Nicole said to herself. "It's probably Squad business."

She answered on the fourth ring. "Hello?" she said.

"May I please speak to Marci Arnold?"

"I'm sorry, she's not here right now. May I take a message?" asked Nicole.

"I saw one of the Super Squad's ads in the bakery. My garden needs some work, and I'd like to hire the Super Squad for the job."

"My name is Nicole Tucker, and I'm a member of the Squad. Can you give me the rest of the details?"

Nicole tried to sound as businesslike as Marci.

"I'm Mr. Clarke, over on Chestnut Street. I'm having an outdoor party for Founder's Day, and my front and back gardens need cleaning up. I know it would have to be done after school and over the weekend—it's maybe a week's worth of work. I'm willing to pay thirty dollars for the job. Are you interested?"

"I sure am! Give me your name and address, and I—I mean *we*—can get started tomorrow."

Nicole quickly took the rest of the information and hung up the phone. She looked around the bedroom, but Marci's old stuffed animals were the only witnesses to the deal she'd just made. "Now we'll have lots of money for the party," she told them triumphantly.

Just then, Marci came in. "Oh, hi, Nicole. What's up?"

"I have the lists for our party." Nicole handed over all her papers. She figured she'd get the bad news over first, then follow up with her good news about the new job.

Marci pushed her glasses up, her brown eyes going wide with shock as she looked over the lists. "Do you realize how much this is going to cost?" she asked.

"I know it's a little more than you'd like," said Nicole, "but—"

"But nothing! You promised me you wouldn't go overboard. Instead, it looks like you're trying to sink

28

the ship!'' Marci waved the lists in her hand. ''We can't afford this.''

''But, Marci—''

''No more 'buts,' '' Marci fumed. ''You just have no idea how to handle money, Nicole. You're so irresponsible!''

''Irresponsible, am I?'' cried Nicole. ''Well, I'll show you, Marci Arnold. You're not the only one who can handle money. I'll organize this party and keep within your miserly budget, you'll see.'' There were tears of rage in Nicole's eyes. ''I'll handle this party myself—finances and all!''

Marci stared at her friend, open-mouthed. ''You'll take care of everything?''

''Sure.'' Nicole nodded. ''And we're going to have the best party ever!'' She headed for the door. ''So just look over those lists and see if there's anything you want to add. I'll take care of the rest.''

She closed the door with a loud bang, then added to herself, ''With a little help from Mr. Clarke, of course.''

Chapter

4

By ten o'clock Saturday morning, each member of the Super Squad was locked away in a room with one of the Williams kids, trying to come up with an idea for a costume. Each one was looking forward to a quick, simple job. After all, it should be easy enough—all they had to do was help a little kid pick a costume, then make it.

"Francine," Carrie called over the noise of the television, "shouldn't you turn that off so we can get to work?"

"Uh-uh," said Francine. "I'm watching to get ideas." She pointed at the cartoon character flying across the screen. "Wonder Beagle is my favorite. Maybe you can make me look like him."

Carrie's heart sank at the thought of building a Wonder Beagle mask. "Maybe."

Francine switched the channel. "Or maybe I could be the Golden Glob. That would be a neat costume."

"But the Golden Glob doesn't have any shape," said Carrie.

"Right," said Francine. "That way nobody would know who I was."

Carrie spread out her pictures. "Want to look at some of my ideas?" she asked.

Instantly, Francine turned off the television and bounced over to her bed. "Yeah, what do you think I should be?"

"How about an alien?" suggested Carrie. She pointed at her picture. "You'd have a mask made out of strips of green crepe paper, with wire antennas sticking out. The body is long, thin pieces of green felt. They swing around like tentacles."

Francine shook her head. "That's kind of gross, if you ask me."

Carrie pulled out another drawing. "How about an Indian princess? You'd have feathers and a brown fringed outfit. If you want, we can even strap a doll to your back as a papoose."

"That sounds like fun," said Francine. "Let's do that one. But I'd like it white, instead of brown."

"Good." Carrie smiled. That costume was a nice, easy one. She'd helped her mother make it for her when she was eight years old. "I think we even have some white material here."

Pinning the costume together on Francine was a

job, though. Carrie wondered if she wiggled so much when she was being fitted.

"Come on, Francine, just hold still for a second."

"I *am* holding still!" Francine jumped up and down. Carrie lost her hold on the material. It fluttered down around Francine's ankles.

Carrie sighed.

"I'm thirsty," said Francine.

"Me, too," Carrie said.

Francine ran to the door. "I'll go get us some juice. You stay and guard the costume." She opened the door and peeked up and down the hallway. "Make sure nobody gets in and steals our idea."

"Okay," said Carrie.

"Betcha I can find out what the other guys are doing." She had a mischievous grin on her face. "I'm a great spy."

"That wouldn't be fair," Carrie said, although she'd love to know what the other girls were coming up with. "We promised to keep our costumes a secret, and we won't cheat."

"Okay," said Francine. She stepped out, then poked her head back in. "I mean, you're sure—"

"I'm sure." Carrie shooed her out. "Just get us some juice."

A couple of minutes later the door opened again. "Francine," said Carrie, "where's the juice?"

"I changed my mind," the little girl said. "Let's look at the pictures." She bounced over to the bed and began riffling through Carrie's sketches.

Carrie shook her head. "But I thought we had decided on the Indian princess."

"Well, yeah. But I wanted to see what else there was." She looked over each sketch, then held one up. "Hey, this is neat. An alien!"

Carrie looked from her sketch to the face grinning up at her. "But you just said this was gross—wait a minute!"

There was a tooth missing in that smile. Carrie gasped. "You're Megan!"

Megan clapped a hand over her mouth and dashed for the door. But she couldn't escape.

No sooner did she open the door, than one of the boys, wearing a red shirt, came tumbling in. Megan crashed into him, and both of them landed on the floor.

Then Francine returned, carrying two glasses of grape juice. "What's going on?" she yelled. "Yikes!"

She tripped over one of the legs wiggling out of the tangle, and the juice spilled all over her brother and sister.

"Look what you did!" howled the boy. "You just ruined my costume!" The tight red shirt he was wearing reminded Carrie of a devil costume Annie had once worn. But now the shirt had a big purple blotch on it.

"You're not supposed to be here, Mike. You were spying!" Megan cried.

Carrie was impressed. Obviously the twins had no trouble telling each other apart.

"And what were *you* doing in Francine's room—visiting?" said Mike.

Francine looked from Megan to the sketches spread out across her bed. "Oh, no! You looked at all our stuff!"

"What's going on out here?" Nicole and Annie were at the door now.

"These two were trying to spy on Francine's costume."

"And they saw everything we were going to do!" Francine added through her tears.

"I'm sorry," said Mike.

"I just wanted a peek," said Megan.

"You ruined *everything*!" Francine sobbed.

Marci joined the group and shook her head. Thank goodness Mrs. Williams was downstairs working in the kitchen. Hopefully she hadn't heard any of this disaster. "Okay, everyone back to their rooms," she ordered.

"We didn't mean to make her cry," said Mike.

"Well, you did. So let's get moving," Annie said.

Everyone left on the double.

Francine dried her eyes as Carrie closed the door. "We have to start all over," the little girl complained, throwing herself on the bed, "because Megan saw all of these."

She picked up Carrie's notebook, and a loose sheet of paper fluttered to the ground. "Hey, what's this?"

"Oh." Carrie grabbed the paper. "That was an idea for my costume."

"What is it?"

"It's a rock star. I was planning on getting a wig and teasing it up, then spraying it with different colors and adding some glitter. The costume would be all black, with colored stones sewn on. Then I was going to wear all different kinds of bracelets, necklaces, and things."

"That sounds really neat," Francine said, putting the sketch down. "I wish I could be that."

Carrie looked down at her young friend thoughtfully. She had wanted a really spectacular costume this year to attract Stevie Winters. Stevie was a big rock fan, and Carrie figured this one-of-a-kind costume would make him notice her. But when she looked at Francine's eager face, she knew she couldn't let the girl down. After all, it wasn't Francine's fault that her brother and sister spied on her and spoiled all her other ideas.

"It's so pretty. Couldn't you make me up like that, Carrie, please?" Francine's lower lip began to quiver.

Carrie shrugged. She'd think of another way to attract Stevie Winters. "Why not? This is an idea nobody has seen. We'll make it for you."

Francine smiled. "Thanks, Carrie. This is going to be great!"

In another room, Marci sat examining a page torn

from a magazine. "You're sure this is what you want?" she asked Doug.

Doug nodded his head vigorously. "As soon as I saw this picture of Ziggie Funk, I knew that's who I wanted to go as. Isn't it neat?"

Marci looked at the picture again. Ziggie was a far-out rock 'n' roller. His face was chalk white, and he had a green star painted around his right eye. His satin suit was green, and so was his electric guitar. "Well, we'll need lots of make-up, and I can probably make the clothes—the only problem is the guitar."

"I've got an old toy banjo," Doug volunteered. "We can spray paint it green." He ran over to his closet and dug the banjo out. "This is going to be great! No one would think I'd pick this kind of costume. It'll be a big surprise!"

Chapter
5

Nicole hummed to herself as she worked. Everything was coming along fine! Megan's costume was just about sewn up. All she had to do was have her try it on one last time and make any final alterations. And this part of the job was working out, too. The glue had finally dried on the long, thin box she'd made out of heavy cardboard. Now she was covering it in bright red paper.

The next step was to glue the panel of black paper to the front, then stick on the gummed address labels she'd gotten from her Mom. When she was finished, the box would look like a real electronic keyboard. Then she'd attach a bright red strap so that Megan could carry it over her shoulder.

A knock at her door made Nicole shove her whole project under the bed. "Who is it?" she called.

"It's Carrie. Your Mom sent me up."

"Okay." Nicole took a quick glance around the room. Good. Nothing about Megan's costume was showing. She opened the door.

"I'm supposed to do the shopping for the decorations," said Carrie as she came in. "Marci said I could pick up the list and the money from you." She looked at Nicole for a long moment. "Is it true? Are you really handling the finances for the whole party?"

"Yeah, I am." Nicole dug through the pile of lists on her desk. "Here's the list of decorations, and here's some money to get them." She dug into the pocket of her jeans and pulled out a few bills. Lucky thing Mr. Clarke had paid her half the fee up front!

"Thanks," said Carrie. "Hey! What happened to your hands?"

Nicole looked down at the Band-Aids on her fingers. She'd started work on Mr. Clarke's yard yesterday and had learned the hard way that you don't pull weeds with your bare hands. Today she'd wear gloves. "Oh, uh, you know, working around the house."

Nicole quickly changed the subject. "So how is your costume coming along for our party? I've decided to be Cleopatra. I'm going to part my hair in the center and wear a tiara made out of gold foil. Maybe I'll stick some fake jewels in it. There's some gold lamé material on sale at the mall that I could make a gown out of. Sound good?"

"Great," said Carrie. "I don't know what I'm going to do. I had an idea—but it didn't work out."

Nicole grinned. "I'll bet you're working on something really gorgeous . . . so that cute Stevie Winters will notice you."

Carrie could feel her cheeks burning. "Nicole!"

Her friend began to laugh. "I thought so!" she crowed. "I've noticed the way you look at him."

Nicole rustled through some papers. "Well, I've been writing down the people we're going to invite. And here he is, right at the top of the list!"

Carrie smiled as she read Stevie's name. "That's great!" Then her smile faded. "But I still don't know what to wear."

"Oh, you'll come up with something," said Nicole. "I'll give you some advice—don't go as a clown."

Carrie gave Nicole a look, but her friend went on. "And don't come as Cleopatra!"

They both laughed. Then Nicole glanced at her watch. "Uh-oh, got to run."

Carrie followed her down the stairs. "Want me to walk you wherever you're going?" she asked.

"Uh, thanks, but you don't have to. I'm kind of in a hurry."

They reached the door, and Carrie watched her friend vanish down the street. "I just don't get it," she whispered to herself. "Nicole is getting as mysterious as Annie!"

Nicole hurried down the street to the Clarkes' house. It was a big old place, set on a double-sized lot. There were two wide lawns and a good-sized garden. Getting it ready for a party would be a lot of work.

An old picket fence in need of a coat of paint surrounded the property. As Nicole opened the gate, she was greeted by loud, excited barking. The Clarkes' dog, a gray mutt named Downboy, came bounding up, his tail wagging. The big, friendly dog immediately lived up to his name. He leaped up, leaning against Nicole, his tongue hanging out. "Down, boy, down," she said, giggling.

The commotion brought Mr. Clarke out onto the porch. He was a tall, skinny man who seemed to have a huge collection of short, baggy slacks. Yesterday's pair had been lime-green. Today's were red, yellow, and purple plaid. He put his hands in his pockets. "Like these?" he asked. "They were a bargain."

He'd said the same thing the day before.

Mr. Clarke looked around the yard. "Where are the other kids?"

"It's just me again, Mr. Clarke," Nicole said. "We've got a lot of jobs to do."

He shook his head. "This seems like quite a job to tackle single-handedly. I wonder if you'll have everything done in time."

"Don't worry about a thing," Nicole assured him. "I'll finish the weeding today. That will just leave mowing the lawn and raking up the cut grass."

"Just remember, you gave me a money-back guarantee. If the yard isn't ready . . . "

"I know, sir," said Nicole, pulling on her gloves. "Well, I'd better get to work."

Mr. Clarke went back inside as Nicole knelt down by the flower beds, pulling up weeds. Downboy stayed out in the yard, running around. Every once in a while he'd come bounding over, wanting to play. Nicole just shooed him off.

She worked her way around flowers and bushes, pulling out weeds and leaving them in little piles in the grass. Downboy sniffed them, shook his head, and dashed away.

Nicole was weeding under the rosebushes when she heard the gate open. When she saw who came through, she ducked down under the bushes. Mrs. Williams! If she mentioned seeing Nicole to the other girls in the Squad, they'd know how Nicole was able to finance the party!

Keeping her face well-hidden, Nicole concentrated on the weeds. It wasn't easy. Her arms caught on thorny branches. Scratches appeared from her elbows to her hands. One of her gloves got caught, and tore open when she ripped it free. But all too soon, the area under the rosebushes was picked clean.

Still Nicole didn't dare move away. She crouched down under the bushes, pretending to pick weeds that weren't there. Mrs. Williams was standing on the porch, right above her, ringing the bell.

Mr. Clarke answered the door.

"Hi, I'm Carol Williams of Carol's Caterers," Mrs. Williams said. "You had called asking about us cooking for your Founder's Day party."

"Well, I don't know if cooking is exactly what we need," said Mr. Clarke. "See, it will be an outdoor party . . . " He led Mrs. Williams along the porch. Nicole's nose nearly touched the dirt as she crouched beneath the bushes.

"This area here will be mowed and cleaned up," Mr. Clarke said. "I have somebody working on that right now . . . "

Please, please, don't call me. Nicole squeezed her eyes tightly shut.

But Mr. Clarke just went on. "We'll have a tent out here, just in case of bad weather."

"Oh, are you renting from Al's Tent-o-Rama?" asked Mrs. Williams.

"Uh, no, I'm borrowing one from my cousin Clyde. It's Army Surplus—olive green may not be the most beautiful color, but it is a bargain."

Nicole rolled her eyes when she heard that.

"So what are you figuring in the way of food?" asked Mrs. Williams. "A buffet? Or do you just want some snack foods then? Cheese puffs, cocktail franks, mini-pizzas?"

"How much would something like that cost?" Mr. Clarke wanted to know. "For say, twenty people?"

Mrs. Williams gave him a price.

"Well, now, I don't know. Sounds a bit pricey to me."

Nicole shook her head. Bargain hunting was one thing, but this was downright *cheap.*

One good thing came of all this. Mrs. Williams was soon walking away from the porch. Nicole raised her head a little bit to watch her leave.

Right then, Downboy came squirming under the bushes. He crept over to Nicole and began licking her face.

"Downboy," she cried, raising her head. "Eek!"

Her hair was caught in the rosebushes!

Chapter
6

Igor's Costume Shop was usually one of the quietest stores in Riverview. Twice a year, though, Igor's was jammed—for Halloween and Founder's Day. Lots of people went there to rent costumes. Others went to get wigs, masks, or make-up.

That's why Marci was in the store—she was buying make-up to turn Doug Williams into Ziggie Funk. She had just put a jar and a make-up crayon on the counter when she noticed Annie standing beside her.

Annie tilted her head to read the cap on the jar. "Clown white?" she said. "Is that what Doug's going to be? A clown? That's not so original."

Marci scooped her stuff up so Annie couldn't see any more. "I thought we agreed not to talk about the costumes we were making."

"I just happened to see the jar. What else do you use clown-white make-up for?"

"I don't know. What do you use old devil costumes for?"

"Well, he's not going to be a devil anymore," Annie giggled. "Not after Francine spilled grape juice all over him." She thought for a second. "A vampire? You'd need a white face for a vampire."

Marci sighed. "I'm not going to tell. What are you buying, anyway?"

Annie quickly hid something behind her back. "I guess you're right. We shouldn't talk about what we're doing."

Shaking her head, Marci paid for her stuff and headed out the door.

That's where she bumped into Nicole.

"What happened to *you*?" Marci asked.

Nicole had Band-Aids on her fingers and thin scratches on her arms and face. Her usually perfect hair looked as if a bird had tried to nest in it. Running an embarrassed hand through the mass of tangles, Nicole said vaguely, "Oh, I guess I had an accident."

Annie came out of the store and stared. But the look Nicole gave her definitely said, "Don't ask."

"I'd almost expect Carrie to show up," Marci joked. "But I guess she's over at school, getting ready for the swim team tryouts."

Clutching the bag with her purchase, Annie glanced at her watch. "I can't believe the time I wasted at the

check-out line!'' she said. "I've got to run. I'm late!''
And she ran off down the street.

Nicole looked at her own watch. "It's really crowded
in there, huh?'' She sighed. "Maybe I'll try and come
back later. I've got to run, too.''

Marci looked at her watch, then shrugged. "Well,
there's no place *I* have to rush off to,'' she said. "But I
wish I knew what was going on around here.''

Annie rushed into school, charging straight for the
locker room. She had wanted to get the purple Mohawk
wig for Mike's costume, but she hadn't counted on
Igor's being so crowded. What if they started the tryouts
before she even got into her suit?

Dashing to a locker, Annie quickly changed.

"There you are, Annie,'' said the slightly plump
coach, Mrs. Samuels. "Just in time.''

She checked off Annie's name on her clipboard and
headed for the pool. Annie followed, trying to swallow
the lump that had suddenly appeared in her throat.

Come on, she told herself. You can do it. You've
worked really hard. You're ready!

Annie stood for a moment beside the locker room,
smelling the warm water and the chlorine. She could
hear rhythmic splashing from the pool. The tryouts had
already begun!

The splashing stopped, and Annie heard a voice call
out, "Great!''

Two swimmers pulled themselves up out of the water.

Annie froze. One of them was Carrie.

Shaking out her blond hair, Carrie suddenly stopped and stared. "Annie!" she called. "What are you doing here?"

"Um—trying out?" she said tentatively. Annie was surprised to hear her voice squeak as she answered.

Carrie grinned. "That's great! You're a super swimmer. All summer I thought of asking you to try out. But you didn't seem interested. Have you been practicing?"

Annie nodded. "At the town pool!"

Carrie's jaw dropped. "So that's where you've been disappearing all this time!" She shook her head. "Why didn't you tell me? We could have practiced together. It would have been a lot more fun." Carrie looked hurt.

"Y-you mean, you don't mind my trying out for the team?" Annie asked.

"Mind?" Carrie looked at Annie as if she had gone crazy. "Why would I mind? I think it would be great, having a friend on the team." She grinned. "Besides, now both of us can be late on account of practice. That's two votes on the Super Squad."

"Annie," Mrs. Samuels called. "It's your turn."

"*If* I make the team," Annie whispered.

"Go and show 'em," said Carrie. "Good luck!"

Annie walked over to Mrs. Samuels by the side of the pool.

"Take your place, Annie," the coach instructed.

With a glance at the girl in the next lane, Annie

stepped to her assigned spot. She forced all thoughts out of her head. This was the moment she'd been working so hard for. Now it was time to see if she could do it.

"I want you to give me four laps, girls. All right. Ready . . . set . . . GO!"

Annie dove into the water and moved forward in a flurry of motion. All her practice took hold, and she sliced smoothly through the water. She could hear the splashing of the next swimmer, but she paid no attention. The far end of the pool was fast approaching.

Taking a deep breath, Annie turned underwater. She hit her rhythm, and the far end of the pool seemed to come up even faster this time. She turned again, and set off on her third lap. Another turn, and then she was heading back to Mrs. Samuels.

She swam the length of the pool, then came breathlessly to a stop. Would she make the team? She climbed out of the pool, watching Mrs. Samuels. But she couldn't read the answer on the coach's face.

Mrs. Samuels studied her stopwatch for a moment, then smiled broadly at Annie as she handed her a large white towel.

"Well, Annie, that was very nice," she said. "Welcome to the Junior Varsity Swim Team."

Carrie broke into a whoop.

"Y-you're kidding?" Annie sputtered. She could feel her heart thudding wildly in her chest.

"You made a very nice time here, and with a little

coaching, you could really improve." Mrs. Samuels smiled. "Practice is at three-thirty, every Monday, Tuesday, and Thursday. Now go change. I don't want my new star fish catching a chill."

Carrie rushed over and gave Annie a hug. "Way to go!" she cried. "Wait till everybody hears about this! We'll really have something to celebrate at the party!"

Annie could feel a happy smile spreading over her face. "You're right," she said. "In fact, now I've finally gotten an idea for my party costume. I'll go as a starfish. What do you think?"

"Perfect!" said Carrie. "You swim like a fish, and you're sure to be a star on the team. I only wish I could get a good idea like that."

They walked off together, grinning.

Marci smiled as she finished her make-up job on Doug. She held up the mirror. "There you are," she said.

"Wow, just like the picture!" said Doug. His face was dead-white, with a green star around his eye. The practice session had taken some time, but it had finally turned out perfect.

"Too bad I can't show the other kids," Doug said, admiring himself.

"They'll see soon enough. Tomorrow is Friday, time for our private show."

Doug grinned. "I can hardly wait."

Marci grinned back. "Neither can I. Now let's get this

55

goop off your face. You don't want to give any clues to your brother or sisters.''

While Doug scrubbed his face, someone knocked at the door. "Who is it?" Marci asked.

"It's Megan," came the muffled reply. "May I come in?"

"Just a minute." Marci gathered up the rest of Doug's costume, then ran a towel over his face. "Okay."

Megan poked her head around the door. "I just wondered if you had seen Nicole."

Marci shook her head. "She's been awfully busy lately. I've hardly even spoken to her."

Megan looked worried. "It's just that I haven't seen her since I tried on my costume. And that was almost a week ago."

"Well, she certainly had lots of time to take care of it, then," said Marci. "You'll see Nicole—and your costume—tomorrow. That's for sure."

But Megan still looked worried. "I hope so," she said.

Chapter 7

It was Friday afternoon, and the Super Squad was having a last-minute meeting at Marci's house before heading over to the Williams's. Each girl carried a big, wrapped bundle—the secret costumes that would finally be revealed.

"Looks like everything is going fine," said Marci. We're all set on the Williams job, and it looks as though our party is all set up—thanks to Nicole."

Nicole managed a weak smile. She looked as though she were having a hard time staying awake.

"No, really," Marci said. "Carrie brought over the decorations, and they look great. And everyone in school is talking about their invitations. I really have to hand it to you, Nicole. You've done a great job."

Nicole smiled and rubbed one of the scratches on her arm.

Marci took a deep breath. "I just wanted to say that—well, I owe you an apology. I didn't think you could handle budgeting for this party, and I was wrong. Everything is going great. So if you need a little extra money from the Millionaire's Fund . . ."

"Uh, no, that's okay." Nicole looked at her watch. "In fact, I really have to go. There are a couple of last-minute details I have to take care of."

"Wait a second," said Annie. "I haven't had a chance to tell you my good news yet." She grinned. "I made the swimming team!"

Everyone cheered for her.

"Let's get some soda," said Carrie. "We should toast our new sports hero."

But Nicole was heading up the stairs. "That's great," she said. "But I've really got to run."

"What about Megan's costume?" Marci asked. "Aren't you bringing it over?"

Nicole rubbed her forehead tiredly. "Right. I forgot about that. Could one of you bring it over? I've just got some stuff to finish. I'll be there in time for the grand costume show, I promise."

Everyone watched her go.

"What's she up to?" Marci asked.

"I don't know," said Carrie.

"Well, one thing's for sure. *She's* not trying out for the swim team."

"I know," said Carrie. "The way she's been looking lately, you'd think she'd joined the jungle survival club."

Marci shrugged. "She'll catch up with us at the Williams's. Now, if I remember right, someone said something about sodas and a toast."

They all headed up to the kitchen.

Nicole hurried along to Mr. Clarke's house. She'd already mowed half of his back lawn. All she had left was to finish the mowing, then rake up the grass cuttings.

She sighed. She felt as though she hadn't had a spare minute in ages. Either she had been working on Megan's costume, or her own, or the party, or Mr. Clarke's yard. It would be nice to sit down and watch television or something, without having to feel guilty about goofing off.

Downboy came bouncing up to greet her, barking his head off as she opened the gate. Then Mr. Clarke appeared on the porch. Today he had lemon-yellow slacks with big pink sailboats on them. "Like 'em?" he asked.

"They look like a real bargain," said Nicole.

Mr. Clarke nodded happily. "Looks like you're just about finished here," he said. "You've really put in a lot of hard work. Where were your helpers?"

Nicole just shrugged. "We all had other jobs. Founder's Day is our busy season."

"Come up and knock on the door when you're done," said Mr. Clarke. "I'll pay you the rest of your money."

He went back inside, and Nicole went around the house to the garage. She returned, pulling the lawn-mower with one hand and carrying a rake in the other. It was a big, old-fashioned square rake, with a long wooden handle.

Leaning the rake against a tree, Nicole went to work with the mower. Half an hour later, the whole lawn was trimmed, with neat rows of grass cuttings lying on the ground. Nicole looked at her watch. She'd have to work fast. The rest of the Super Squad would soon be arriving at the Williams house.

Nicole grabbed the rake and began raking the cut grass. Soon she had a big pile. She stood over it for a second, then slapped herself on the forehead. "I must really be getting tired," she said to herself. "I forgot to bring something to put the grass in!"

Then she remembered the old bushel basket in the garage. That would do just fine. Dropping the rake, she raced back around the house.

She was carrying the basket back to the lawn when she saw Downboy running ahead of her. He turned and watched, his pink tongue hanging out, his tail wagging madly. Then he ran off into the back yard.

Nicole rushed up to find Downboy barking with delight at the mound of raked grass. He put his head down and charged right into it. Grass sprayed every which way.

"Oh, *no!*" said Nicole. "Downboy! Stop it!"

But Downboy didn't stop. He turned around,

preparing for another charge at the grass pile.

Nicole dropped her basket and ran forward, waving her arms. "Downboy! No! Bad dog!"

She had almost reached Downboy when her foot hit something hard. Too late, she realized what it was. The rake! She tried to stop. But the handle was already swinging up to hit her . . . .

Marci sat on Mrs. Williams's blue-flowered couch, looking at her watch. "Nicole told us she'd be here," she said. "I can't imagine what's keeping her."

Mrs. Williams shook her head. "I don't know if my devils will be able to wait much longer."

The Williams twins were running around the coffee table, getting wilder by the minute. "We want our costumes! We want our costumes!" they chanted.

Mike ran over to his mother. "Mommy, do we have to wait for Nicole?" It was about the fiftieth time that one of the kids had asked that question.

"I know how to put my costume on," Megan said, trying to hide her disappointment. "I don't need Nicole to help me, you know."

"Well, maybe I can help you if you need it," her mother volunteered. "And Nicole can see you all dressed up when she gets here. She can see all of you."

The kids all cheered, and Marci threw Mrs. Williams a grateful look. "Okay, kids, it's settled. Everyone upstairs," she ordered.

The twins thundered up the stairs, but Mike stopped halfway up. "But no peeking," he said. "We've kept it secret up to now. So let's keep it that way."

Marci waited until the kids had disappeared, then followed them up more slowly. "I think Doug will need a little help from me," she said.

"Francine may need some last-minute adjustments," said Carrie.

Annie went to check on Mike, and Mrs. Williams followed to see if Megan needed help.

A short while later, they were all downstairs again. "Everybody ready up there?" called Mrs. Williams.

"READY!" came the four answers.

"Okay, kids," said Mrs. Williams.

The stampede of feet could be heard in the hallway overhead. Then the racket reached the top of the stairs and roared into the living room. The four kids raced in, eyes bright with excitement. They were so busy running, they hadn't even taken the time to look at each other's costumes.

Doug was the first to look around at the others. "Oh, no!" he bellowed. "I can't believe it!"

He put his hands on the hips of his green satin Ziggie Funk costume. His green guitar hung from one shoulder. Francine stood in her black jumpsuit with the fake jewels sparkling, a red, pink, and orange wig on her head. In her hand she held a shiny aluminum-foil microphone.

Mike wore a red shirt with purple splotches, with matching purple pants and red boots. A fake Mohawk haircut with purple hair rose off his head, and a whole tiny drum set hung from his shoulders.

Megan was wearing a tuxedo with tails. Red glitter covered the lapels of her jacket and the line down the seams of her pants. She had a red-glitter bow tie, and red glitter sparkled on the band of the battered high hat on her head. Slung over her shoulder on a red sash was a make-believe organ keyboard.

All the kids stared at each other in amazement.

"We're all rock stars!" Mike burst out. "How could that happen?"

"Doug picked his Ziggie Funk costume out of a picture," said Marci.

"And Francine and I worked from the only sketch that nobody else had seen," said Carrie. "That was going to be *my* costume."

"We got our idea after Mike had the grape juice spilled on him," said Annie.

"Nicole showed me this neat tuxedo in one of her fashion magazines," said Megan. "I thought it looked like a rock star's outfit!"

"That's great," moaned Mike, throwing himself into a chair. "What are we going to do? I told everyone we'd be coming in different costumes this year."

"Me, too," said Francine.

The other Williamses agreed.

"Well, the parade is tomorrow," Carrie said unhappily. "There's just no time to make new costumes. Look how long it took to make these."

"We're going to look dumb if we go dressed like this," said Doug.

"If Doug's not going, I'm not going," said Megan.

"Come on, kids," Marci pleaded. "You've got to go. Think of all the fun you'll miss."

"Well, maybe," said Francine.

"I do like parades," said Mike.

Reluctantly, all the kids agreed to go.

"At least that's settled," said Mrs. Williams with relief.

Just then, the doorbell rang.

"That must be Nicole," said Marci, going to answer it. "She missed all the excitement."

She opened the door and gasped when she saw her friend's face.

"Nicole!" Marci shouted. "You've got a black eye!"

Chapter
8

Nicole came into the house and began to cry.

"I'll get some ice for that eye," said Mrs. Williams.

"Sit down," said Annie.

"What happened?" Carrie wanted to know.

"I t-took a job on the side." Nicole sobbed. "To pay for the party."

Mrs. Williams brought out some ice cubes wrapped in cloth. As Nicole gingerly pressed them to her glowing shiner, she told the whole story.

"You took a job—and didn't tell us?" said Marci. "That's against the rules of the Super Squad."

"You made me so mad, Marci, when you called me irresponsible that I wanted to prove to you I could handle this party. So I took this job to cover the extra expenses."

"I understand why you did it," Annie said sympathetically. "I know what it's like to want to prove yourself."

"But you should have come to us," said Carrie. "We're a team!"

Nicole nodded in agreement, then looked at Marci. Marci was upset. "You shouldn't have lied to us, Nicole," she said. "But I shouldn't have called you irresponsible either. Do you forgive me?" All the girls knew how hard it was for Marci to admit she was wrong—about anything.

Nicole smiled at her friend and gave her a quick hug.

Then Marci's practical streak took over. "So, did you get paid?"

Nicole shook her head. "I knew I wouldn't finish on time, and I gave Mr. Clarke a money-back guarantee. So when the rake hit me on the head, I just ran out of there." She had finally stopped crying and looked around for Megan.

"I'm sorry I wasn't here to help you get dressed, Megan," she said. "But your costume looks perfect."

"That's okay," Megan replied generously. "Only look at us."

For the first time, Nicole looked at all four Williamses. "Oh, no . . . but—"

"We know." Carrie sighed. "But I think we've worked through that problem. Now we have to take care of yours."

Downboy was delighted to discover three new playmates as the Super Squad worked to clean up the lawn. He raced around them in circles, barking his head off.

Mr. Clarke stepped onto the porch. "Glad to see poor Nicole finally got some help," he said. "This was a pretty big job for one person to tackle alone." He glanced over to her. "Letting her rest under the tree, eh?"

"Right," said Marci. "She did enough."

Mr. Clarke went back inside. Nicole let out a long sigh, pressing a new piece of ice against her black eye.

Then Downboy romped over and leaped onto her, sending her toppling. Nicole sputtered and thrashed around as Downboy licked her face.

"I think he likes you," Annie giggled.

Nicole made a face. "With friends like him . . ."

The girls soon finished the job and collected their pay. "This will take care of the party goodies," said Marci. "With a little help from the Millionaire's Fund we'll buy some tonight, and—uh-oh."

"What's wrong?" asked Annie.

"I'll have to finish up my costume tonight, too," Marci explained. "Doug's costume took up so much of my time, I haven't finished my own."

"Tell me about it!" groaned Carrie. "I haven't even been able to think of a costume. Maybe I'll just wear a jogging shirt and shorts and go as a runner."

"I've got a better idea," said Nicole. "I got a gold lamé dress—that I won't be using."

"Why not?" asked Carrie.

70

Nicole took away her ice pack. "Cleopatra with a shiner?" She shook her head. "I've got another idea. But you can use my dress, and the high sandals I was going to wear."

"Me? As Cleopatra?" Carrie looked dubious. "I don't think so, Nicole."

"How about a runner?" Nicole suggested. "A runner from the original Olympics? You could cut my gown into one of those short Greek tunic things. I even have some red sparkle glue to make designs on it. And the gold foil I was going to use for a crown could be your Olympic torch."

Carrie nodded. "That sounds fantastic. But what will you wear?"

Nicole smiled mysteriously. "Something that will hide my black eye."

"I've got an old gorilla mask at home," Annie offered.

They all laughed.

The next morning, the members of the Squad all met at Marci's house before going to the parade.

"Carrie!" squealed Annie. "You look incredible!"

Carrie looked down a bit self-consciously at her costume. "Are you sure it's all right?"

"All right? You look like one of those Greek statues, come to life!"

The short tunic showed off Carrie's slim figure and long legs, especially with the straps of the high sandals climbing to her knees. Every time she moved, the gold material glittered in the sun. A thin red headband held back her hair, matching the red pattern at the hem of her skirt. The gold-foil torch completed the costume.

"Well, you don't look so bad yourself," said Carrie, admiring Annie's outfit. She was wearing a blue bathing suit, with bright yellow cloth starfish sewed on. Perched on her head, beret-fashion, was a five-armed starfish hat. And from her waist she wore a starfish skirt, with five pleated arms sticking out.

"I just wonder how Nicole will hide—"

"Avast!" cried a voice from behind them.

They turned to see Nicole standing there, wearing black pants with high black boots, a red satin shirt, and a gold vest. A red silk scarf covered her hair—and a black eyepatch covered her shiner. She waved an aluminum-foil sword at them. "What do you think, my friends? Nicole Tucker, Pirate Princess!"

"Pretty neat!" said Carrie.

"Yeah, you even hid your black eye!" said Annie.

The only one who's hiding right now is Marci," said Nicole. "Where is she?"

Right then, the door to the house opened, and Marci stepped out. "Sorry," she said. "My costume is going to take a few more minutes."

Everyone stared at her. She was just wearing shorts and a T-shirt. "Doesn't look like much of a costume to me," said Carrie.

Marci grinned. "Come on inside before you say that."

72

They walked into the living room to find a big cardboard box on its side. The box had been painted silver, with lots of buttons and dials glued onto it. Tiny light bulbs stuck out here and there. It looked like a giant computer.

Marci crawled into the box. "Just a couple more wires to connect . . . ." Her voice come out muffled from the cave-like box. ". . . And some more batteries."

She pulled at the box till it stood upright. Then her head popped out through a hole in the top. The box covered her from her shoulders to her knees. "See?" she said. "Now, when I push these buttons inside here, watch what happens."

Lights began flickering all over her costume.

"Neat!" said Carrie.

Marci's smile got bigger. "There's even a little shelf inside here for extra batteries. I thought of everything."

"*Almost* everything," said Nicole.

"What do you mean?" Marci demanded.

"Let me shake hands with you over this great costume." Nicole stuck out her hand.

Above the silver box, Marci's face went bright red. "Oh, no!" she wailed. "No armholes!"

"And no time to cut them now," said Annie, looking at her watch. "The parade is about to begin!"

The green square of Riverview Park was surrounded by a large, colorful crowd of adults as well as children.

Everybody dressed up for Founder's Day, and whole families took part in the parade.

"Look over there!" said Carrie. "I don't believe it!" One family had come as a home entertainment center. Dad was a TV set, with his head peering out of the screen. Mom was a stereo, wearing a big box with a transistor radio hidden inside to provide the sound. The two children were speakers, attached to their mother by coils of wire.

Marci sighed. "At least they remembered to cut armholes."

They passed a man in a cheap rubber mask and a pair of pink-and-purple baggy pants. Nicole began to giggle. "That's Mr. Clarke. I'd know those pants anywhere. What do you want to bet that his mask was a bargain?"

They finally found the Williams kids huddled around their mother, looking miserable.

"My devils are all in terrible moods," said Mrs. Williams. "They don't want to march past the judges' stand."

At the far end of the park was a reviewing stand, where judges made notes for the Thaddeus Parker Awards for best costumes.

"They'll laugh at us," Mike said.

"Come on, kids, cheer up," said Annie. "Your costumes all look super. And see how good everyone else looks."

"Yeah," said Doug, looking at his shoes. "But they're not all dressed alike."

"Remember, *you* were the one who chose to be Ziggie Funk. Do you see something here you'd rather be?" asked Marci.

Doug looked at a boy dressed as a headhunter, with shrunken heads dangling around his neck. Then came a man disguised as a whale. Every once in a while, a spray of water erupted from his costume. Doug stared around, but finally shook his head. "No, I *like* being Ziggie Funk."

"And I like my costume," said Megan, watching the sunlight sparkle off her red glitter.

"Me, too," said Francine. "I want to win a prize."

"We'll never win," said Mike.

"Don't be so sure," said Annie.

Mike looked up. "You think I could?" A hopeful smile lit up his face.

"There's only one way to find out," said Nicole. "That's by marching past the judges."

"What are we waiting for?" The kids cheered.

Everyone had a wonderful time marching in the parade. They all "ooohed" and "aaaahed" at the costumes and laughed a lot. By the time they reached the judges' stand, Nicole had them singing a silly song about pirates.

When the parade was over, everyone gathered by the judges' stand to hear the winners.

Mrs. Edwards was the principal of Riverview Junior High and the head judge. She tapped on the microphone and said, "First, I'd like to say that everyone in the parade looked like a winner. Old Thaddeus would be proud of you all. We had a very hard choice to make. So let's have a round of applause for all the costumes."

The audience clapped enthusiastically.

"And we don't have any single winners this year," Mrs. Edwards went on. "We have two very clever group costumes. In the adult category, the prize goes to the car. Let's get all those fellows up here to accept their ribbon."

People murmured in surprise as about twenty guys from the local college came out of the crowd. Some were dressed as wheels. Marci saw one who wore a hat like a headlight.

A boy with a steering wheel on his chest shouted, "One, two, three!" The boys ran together, bent down, linked arms—and in a few seconds transformed themselves from separate parts into an entire car!

Everyone burst into applause when they saw that.

Mrs. Edwards looked at her notes. "Charlie Andrews was the one with the original idea, so I'll hand the ribbon to him. But congratulations to all the parts!"

The audience laughed as the boy with the steering wheel came up to take the prize.

"Great costume," said Mrs. Edwards. "And now, for our children's category, we have another joint winner. Will the rock group please come out?" She looked expectantly out into the crowd.

No one came

Mrs. Edwards consulted her list. "The rock group, please? Francine, Megan, Mike, and Doug Williams?"

A disbelieving squeal broke out behind the Super Squad. Then the Williams kids ran up to the judges' stand. The audience laughed and clapped when they saw the kids together.

"I don't know whether I should ask them to sing or give an acceptance speech," joked Mrs. Edwards as she handed them their ribbon.

All the kids said, "Thanks, Super Squad."

The girls all looked at each other. "Well, what do you know?" said Nicole. "We *all* won."

The kids came charging back to hug the Squad members. "We did it! We did it!" they screamed.

"You sure did," said Mrs. Williams, throwing her arms around her children. She smiled at the Squad and winked. "You sure did."

The crowd began breaking up. "Well, that does it," said Annie. "Now all we have to worry about is our party—and having a good time."

"Um, right," Carrie answered. She was up on tiptoe, looking this way and that among the crowd. All during the parade, she'd been looking for Stevie. And she hadn't seen him at all.

A crowd of yelling kids came running past, and she stepped back, banging into someone. She turned around, and found herself looking at a shower

curtain. It was covered with ducks in rain gear, and ran around a circular piece of wire attached to a stick. The person inside held the stick, and every once in a while blew bubbles out the top of his "shower stall."

"Oh, sorry," said Carrie.

"Hey, that's a great costume."

The curtain opened, and a face appeared—Stevie Winters!

He smiled. "I'm really looking forward to seeing you tonight at the party. I've been washing up all day!"

"Yeah—yeah, me, too," said Carrie. "I mean, I'll see you at the party." She ran after her friends as if she were walking on air. This *was* going to be a great party!

Chapter
9

"*Super* party!" Annie called to Nicole across the crowd.

Marci's basement was filled with kids rocking to the beat of the stereo in the corner. Streamers and decorations had completely changed the look of the room. Two big tables groaned under the weight of sodas and snacks.

Annie carefully balanced two glasses of soda in her hands as she squirmed her way through the crowd over to Nicole.

"Remind me, next time we have a party, I'd better invite fewer people," said Nicole. "There's hardly enough air in here to breathe."

"You mean, cut down on some of the cute boys?" Annie teased.

Nicole grinned. "No. But there must be some way to invite fewer girls." She looked at the soda in Annie's hands. "Going to share that with one of the guys?"

Annie shook her head. "Actually, it's for Marci."

They looked over in the corner of the room, where Marci was talking with Bobby Cahill, looking longingly at the soda in his hand.

"Tough break," Nicole said, laughing. "The way she wired up those lights, there's no way she could cut any armholes without cutting the wires." She shook her head. "The things we do for beauty."

"Anyway, I've promised to bring her a drink," said Annie.

"We'll take turns." Nicole leaned closer, grinning at her friend. "But don't count on Carrie to help much. She's spending most of the night dancing with a shower stall."

Annie grinned back. "That's no ordinary shower stall. That's Stevie Winters."

"Well, I always said, she had great taste in shower stalls." Nicole sighed and ran a finger against the edge of her eyepatch. "Just think, I might have been Cleopatra, barging around here tonight. If I hadn't stepped on that stupid rake and . . ."

"Hey, Nicole?" A really cute boy stepped over to them. "I just heard that you're wearing that eyepatch for real! Is that true?"

Nicole looked up pitifully at him. "Yes, it is," she said. "Just look what happened to me!" she flipped the patch up.

"Gosh, that's terrible!" The boy stepped closer to look at her black eye. "How did you get a shiner like that?"

"Oh, it's a long story . . ." Nicole glanced back at Annie and winked her good eye as she walked off with the boy.

Annie shook her head. "If she hadn't stepped on that stupid rake . . ."

She went back to pushing her way through the crowd until she made it to Marci's side.

"Finally!" Marci whispered. "I thought I was going to die of thirst." She looked at Annie, a little embarrassed. "Um, could you hold it up for me?"

Annie held up the glass, and Marci took a long sip. "Oh, that tastes so good. Thanks a lot, Annie." She took another sip, then said, "I don't know how I could have been so stupid. Designing a costume like this, with no way to use my arms!"

"There's always next year," Annie reminded her.

Marci nodded. "Next Founder's Day, I'm going with something simple and easy." She thought for a second. "Maybe a fortune teller. I'll wear a Gypsy blouse, a shawl, and a nice floral skirt. I could carry a crystal ball and look into the future for people."

"That's a great idea!" Annie teased. "And after the holiday, you could keep the crystal ball. With that to guide our investments, our Millionaire's Fund should break a million in no time."

Marci gave her a look. "Ha, ha. Very funny." She

looked around at the party. "At least this bash didn't ruin the Fund."

Annie glanced at her. "You're not still—you know—upset with Nicole, are you? For taking the job to pay for the party?"

"I was—for about ten seconds." Marci admitted. "But she worked so hard, on her own time. And she certainly did a good job on Megan's costume, too. If she wanted to use the money for a party, I guess that's all right." She giggled. "Besides, I don't think she'd do it again. At least, not on a job where she's got to work around Downboy. I think for once, she's learned her lesson."

Annie glanced over to where Nicole and her new friend were talking. "Oh," she said, a slow grin tugging at her lips, "I don't think she's doing too badly right now."